When Sophie's Feelings Are Really, Really Hurt

BY MOLLY BANG

THE BLUE SKY PRESS
An Imprint of Scholastic Inc. • New York

Sophie loves to paint. She also loves the woods. Now Ms. Mulry is telling the class: "After school, find a tree you like a LOT. Look at it carefully—the trunk, the branches, the leaves. Tomorrow you're going to paint that tree from memory."

Sophie already has
a favorite tree:
a big beech in the
woods by her house.

Whenever she feels angry
or sad, she climbs this
tree, and her anger and
sadness melt away.

Sophie feels good just walking
toward her tree.

Her breathing is deep and slow.

She looks at the beech tree
carefully.

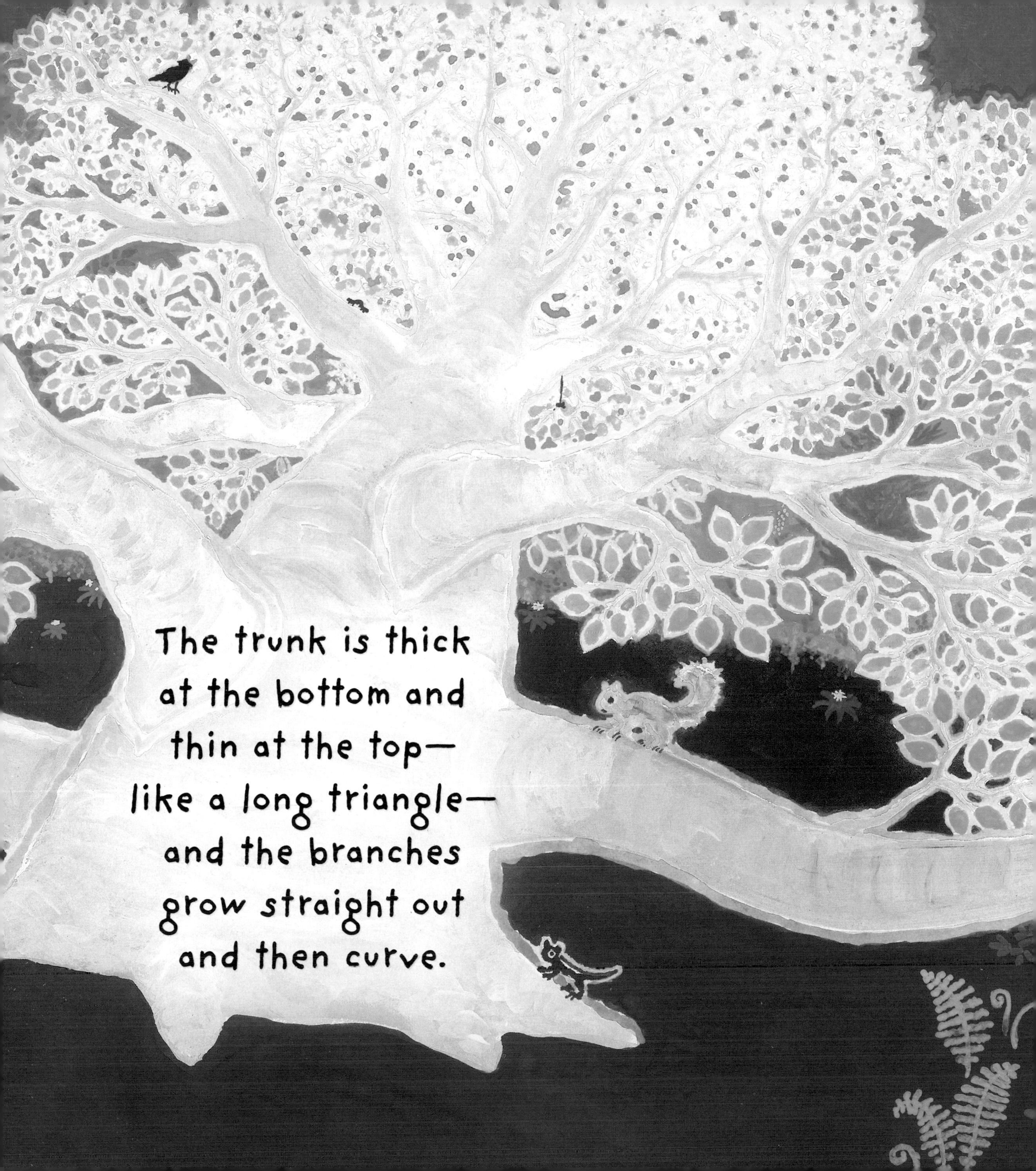

The trunk is thick
at the bottom and
thin at the top—
like a long triangle—
and the branches
grow straight out
and then curve.

As she climbs, Sophie feels the smooth bark under her hands. She looks closely at the bark, the branches, and the leaves. When she looks up, the leaves glow in the sun.

Sophie sits on a high branch and holds the trunk, memorizing everything. She climbs down and carries her memories home.

In school the next day,
Sophie is excited.
She knows her
painting will show
how much she loves
the tree. She can
see it in her mind.

But when she paints
the trunk gray, it
looks dull and sad.
It feels all wrong.

My tree isn't sad
at all! Sophie thinks.
What can I do?

YOGURT

She paints her tree
turquoise blue.

Wow.
Not sad anymore!

But now she has
another problem:

If the tree is blue,
what color is the sky?

Sophie paints the sky orange.
Now the tree pops right out.
The beech looks wonderful—
the way it makes her feel.

But plain green leaves look too dark.

Sophie remembers how each leaf
glowed in the sun. She tries yellow and
mixes in some green. She even knows
this color's name: chartreuse. YES!

How can she make the tree still more wonderful? She paints yellow all around it, as if it's shining. She fills her shining tree with animals she has seen in the woods.

OH,
IS SOPHIE
EVER HAPPY NOW!

Andrew looks over at her painting. "Sophie, your tree is WRONG," he says. "Real trees aren't blue!"

Other children move closer to see.

"You made a goofy ORANGE SKY, too!" Andrew says. Everyone starts to giggle.

"We're supposed to paint a REAL tree, Sophie. You did it WRONG."

YOGURT

Sophie feels her face get hot. She stares down at her sneakers. She feels tears dribbling down her cheeks.

She wants to JUST NOT BE THERE. Everybody is giggling and whispering.

Why did she do it all WRONG?

She hates her picture. She hates to paint!

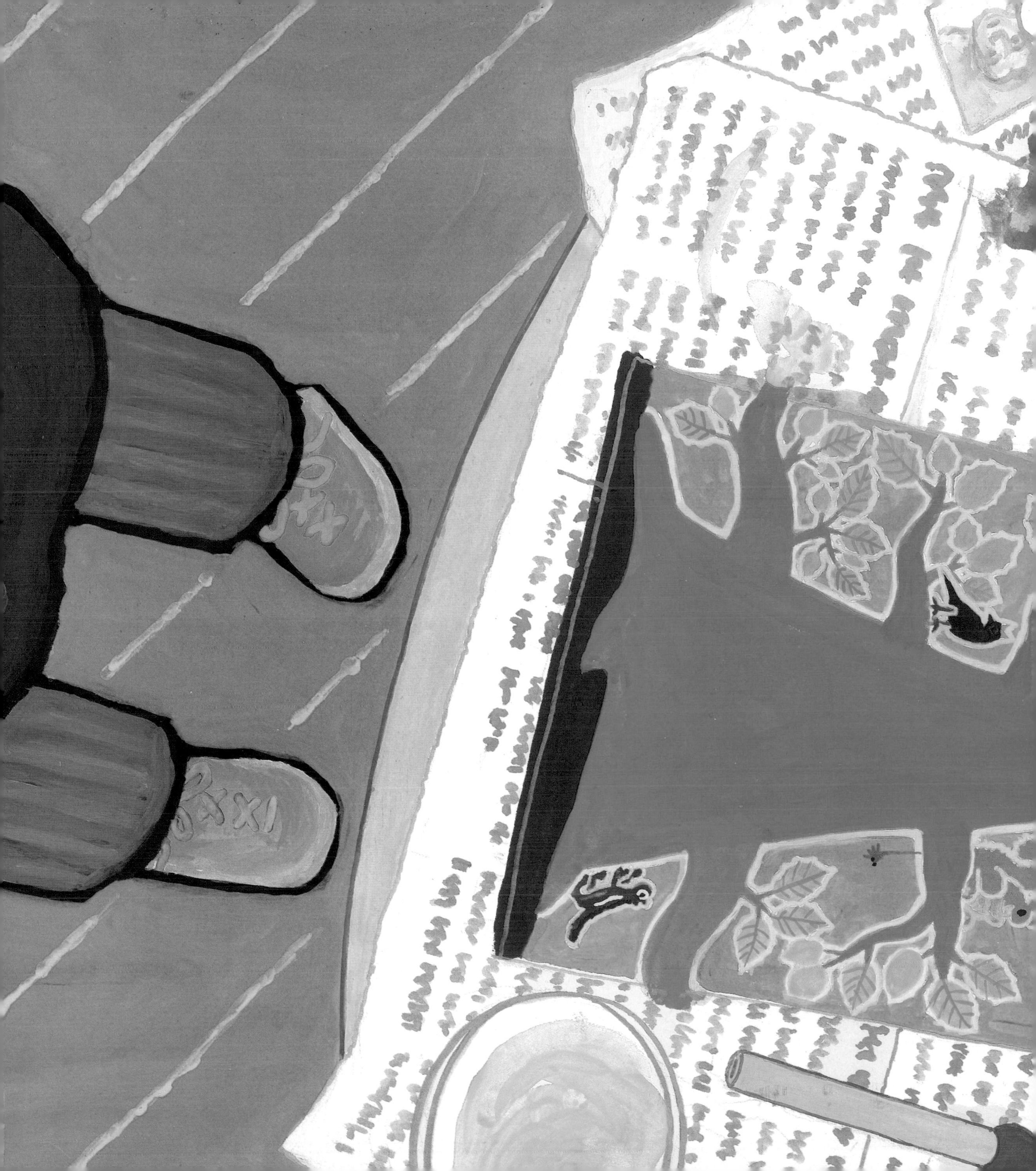

Suddenly Ms. Mulry is there.

"What's happening,
Sophie?" she asks.

"She did it wrong!" says Andrew. "She made it all weird colors."

Ms. Mulry smiles. "Sophie, tell us about your painting," she says.

"It's my favorite tree," Sophie mumbles. "I did look at everything, just like you said. The branches go straight out and curvy, and the leaves are all jaggedy. I tried painting the trunk gray, but it looked too sad."

Sophie's voice gets stronger.

"So I painted it bright blue because that's how it makes me FEEL."

"How is that?" asks Ms. Mulry.

"It makes me feel . . . good. And strong."

"Yes," says Ms. Mulry.
"When I look at your
picture, I feel that, too."

She holds up Sophie's painting for the class to see. "This is a beech tree, isn't it, Sophie?"

Sophie nods. She feels better.

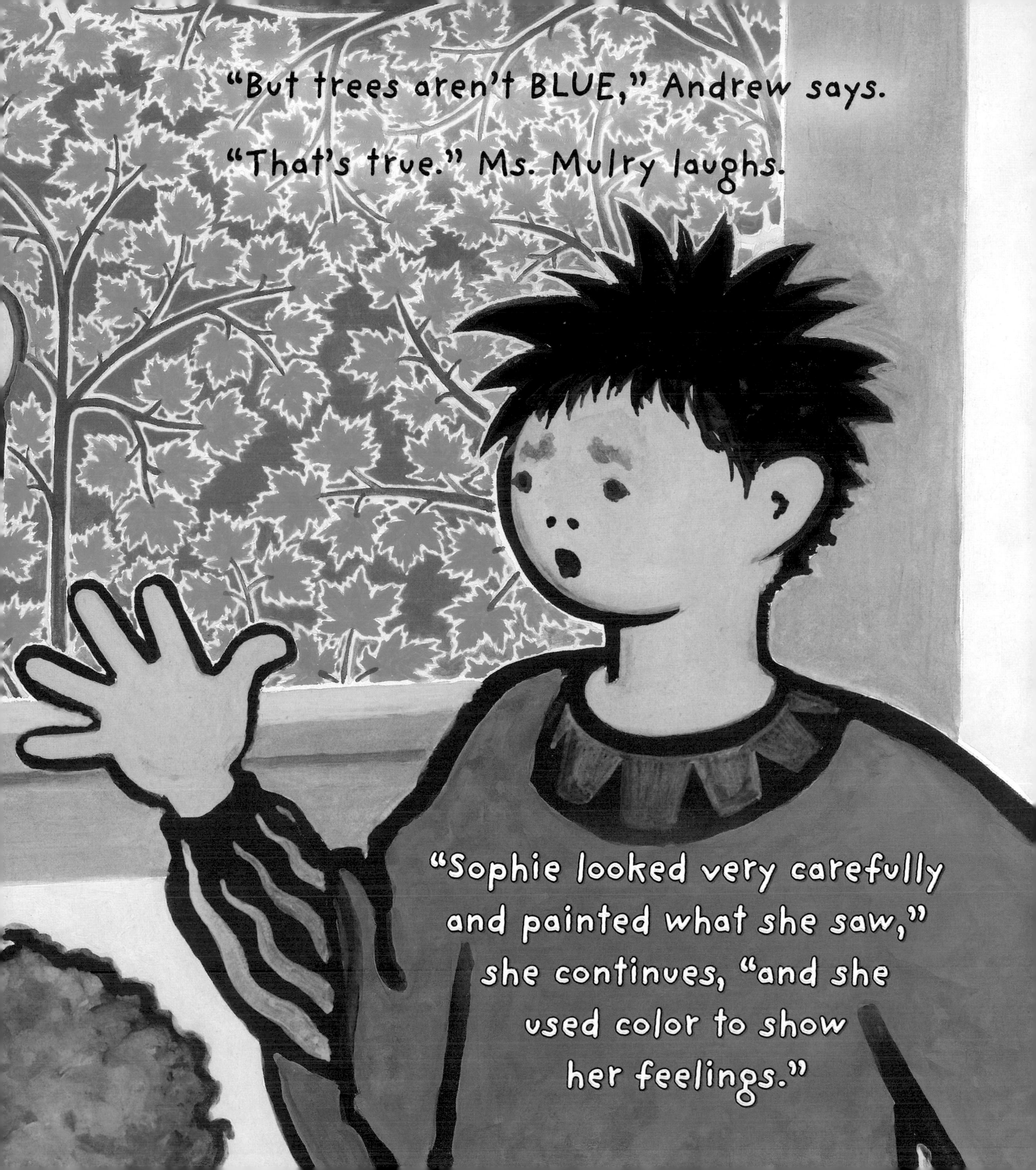

“But trees aren’t BLUE,” Andrew says.

“That’s true.” Ms. Mulry laughs.

“Sophie looked very carefully and painted what she saw,” she continues, “and she used color to show her feelings.”

"Tell us about your picture, Andrew," says Ms. Mulry.

"It's a pine tree," Andrew says. "It's twisty, with patchy bark. The pine needles are sharp and poky."

Sophie points at the roots. "His tree is holding on to the hill like it will never let go—ever."

"Yes," says Ms. Mulry. "Perhaps that shows some of Andrew's feelings about his tree."

She holds up the two pictures.

"Both artists
looked carefully at their trees and made
very different—and very special—paintings."

"Now let's put all the paintings on the floor. Find something special and different in every one—maybe something you want to use the next time you paint."

Sophie looks at her painting for a long time. Andrew looks at it, too. "Your blue tree does look kind of happy," he says.

"And I like how your tree holds on tight," Sophie replies.

After school,
Sophie walks to her
beech tree, but she doesn't feel angry
or sad or hurt anymore.
Sophie loves painting,
and she loves her tree.

And she loves
just being Sophie.

TO BELOVED

Chloe, David, Eloise, Izzy, Julia, Juliet, Lee, Sagan, Sundiata,
and still and always Monika.

Everyone has hurt feelings sometimes, and people do different things to feel better. Sometimes talking to a trusted friend is helpful, or we might share our feelings with a teacher or parent. It also helps when we make an extra effort to be sure we don't hurt the feelings of others.

What do you do when your feelings are hurt?

THE BLUE SKY PRESS

Library of Congress catalog card number 2014043593

ISBN 978-0-545-78831-1

10 9 8 7 6 5 4 3 2 1 15 16 17 18 19 20

Printed in Malaysia 108
First edition, October 2015

Book design by Kathleen Westray